I0581559

BOOKS & SMITH
New York Editors

THROUGH THIS STRANGE WINDOW

EDGAR SMITH

SHORT STORIES

A Books&Smith Press publication.

To
Eduardo Lantigua and José M. de la Rosa,
who often offered me their smiles and referred
to me as Storyteller and Poet, respectively.

To Rubén Sánchez Féliz, Kianny N. Antigua,
Ángel Arias, Gisela Vives, and Pedro Santana,
for the multiple inspirations,
for knowing how to really read
and how to separate friendship from reading.

OTHER BOOKS BY THE AUTHOR

El palabrador
Algunas tiernas imprecisiones
Island boy
La inmortalidad del cangrejo
Cuentos raros
Randomly, a poem
Versenal
The Wordsmith
Gnuj & Alt
arrimao
Tandava
Puro cuento
Verso y Lágrima
Voz propia / Voice of our own

WORDS FROM THE AUTHOR:

Prior to the adoption of literature as an escape mechanism (before literature chose to use *me* as a test tube), the idea of my identity—of my physiognomy, of the self, that derives from my appearance always intrigued me. At an early age, I would look at myself in the mirror and think with a certain impatience that, if this strange object did not exist, if water did not exist, humankind would have no way of contemplating their own countenance. I wouldn't know what I look like—which in some way amounts to the notion of not having any appearance at all. Who would I be if I couldn't see my own face?

With this concept in mind, I decided to follow mirrors through the paths of the written word. In a game of cat and mouse, from Dorian Gray (that painting was an infernal mirror), the Gorgon who sees her own face in Perseus's shield, through Narcissus who falls in love with himself until he's consumed by the internal fire of his despair, or the servile mirror of the witch in Snow White, to its numerous mentions by Jorge Luis Borges, the arcane devices haunt me. And I, them. Who hasn't been even momentarily terrified of their own reflection in the dark? Who has not sensed *the other* behind the edges of that crystalline surface?

When I conceived the idea of a collection of stories with the mirror at its backbone—where to explore metaphysical and philosophical questions, as well as to entertain supernatural theories—, when I first imagined the mirror as a curious and mysterious window, another idea immediately struck me: that mirrors and Death coincide at various points. The first mutual characteristic would be their inevitability: we find them everywhere and where we least expect them. They are mysterious and relentless, and seem to embrace the world effortlessly and with no regards for men. Death could very well be a reflection (however distorted) of life, or perhaps an inverted mirror, in which others see themselves, but with different faces: ours.

I imagine, macabrely, that, at the moment of death, instead of crossing a river or a gate, we will open our eyes before a huge mirror, and, in it, we will see our faces, not as we have seen them until now, but as they really are, already devoid of the limiting flesh and bone, but returned to their essence, to the primal matter.

There, we will see our true selves, neither dead nor alive, but essentially naked (of adjectives and preconceptions); and move we will on to another plane, where light and shadow are not at all different.

In the end, other strange, but everyday things crept in between the reflections and the dead, to create a sort of fantastic compendium of objects and thoughts made common by force of habit, but which, if one thinks of them objectively, also have their own mysteries and fictions: books, entities, beings from other planets, perceptions, hell, and the destinies of women and men are some of the concepts I include to accompany Death and mirrors in this intimate narrative journey. It is not hard for me to fathom that, at some point/place in the cosmos, in another dimension, someone with my exact face has written these same stories.

Edgar Smith October 19th, 2020.

Primordial dread

They knew very little then. They did distinguish, even without the benefit of language, the bird from the serpent. They had come to understand the need to flee from certain animals. They knew about fruits—they helped to calm the devouring urge in their insides.

Most of them had just discovered predation as a means of survival. Very few, perhaps the most curious, had already begun the instinctive rite of erection and rubbing.

Since everything was recent, thirst surprised them. And something, which words could never name, impelled them to the river.

In some way, it is valid to say it was thirst that *shaped* mankind: when the fundamental need pushed them to the stream, they saw their faces on the water for the very first time.

The initial reaction was dread. Then, probably, a giggle—swiftly followed by the most elemental laughter. Perhaps, out of sheer emotion, they also cried.

Later, when the waters had become but a regular mirror and mankind had grown used to their own reflection, gradually: vanity, purpose, gods, and philosophy were conceived.

Mirror in the right angle

More than once did I peer into an old mirror which used to adorn the narrow hallway from the kitchen to my room.

I chose a precise time: the twilight on Wednesdays.

At first, I told myself it'd been a fortuitous choice. Then, I thought it a capricious one. After a while, I conceded that it had been circumstantial: it was the sunset that attracted me; how the sun would sink into the horizon with a certain beautiful agony which in time gave the narrow corridor a frolic of glows and shadows. The mirror, sooty and orangey with sunset, gave my reflection from that angle a strange and enticing hue—sepia, I'd say—which enchanted me.

That's all there was to it. Under its spell, which lasted only a few minutes, my eyes contemplated that other man with a familiar face who, in the gloom, seemed sometimes to want to say something and other times to inhabit the most concrete silence.

I condescended occasionally, I must admit, to fantasy: I thought, as I looked at myself, that my reflection was, indeed, another man—someone who had stolen my face. I laughed. I came to imagine him in the bustle of his own life in this other ghostly, repeated world of his; came to think with brief trepidation that perhaps *I* was the obedient reflection of this man, tied to the illusion of my free will, when, in reality, I was returning to this place, at this precise hour, because *he* decided so.

The mirror is gone now. I had to break it. The usual minutes had passed that evening, you see, and the corridor had filled with shadows. I wanted to go, but something stopped me. As the flat surface darkened, in shock, I watched my face disappear. A gradual horror seized me: I thought then that this man was me, truly *me*; and the only thing keeping my essence from vanishing was the possibility of seeing myself in the mirror, in any mirror. I understood then that, without the mirror, without the mimetic power of this object, I would not know who I am: nobody could confirm their own appearance. It would be impossible without these elements to say we know ourselves fully because there would be no natural way of seeing one's own face.

Fear won me over. I struck out blindly and immediately felt a trickle of blood down my wrist. I ran, ran away, as fast as I could. And as I tried to escape, in more than one store display glass I saw my face again... though at that point, I no longer knew who that man was who returned my gaze.

Vis-à-vis

A man is standing in front of me. Just as tall as I am. He arches, like me, his right eyebrow. His hand, which holds a pen similar to the one I'm holding (*or is it the same pen?*), trembles, just like mine. If I were not on this side, I would say this man is me. Surely, as a joke of existence, he may be thinking that I am a man similar to him; and were he on this side, no one would be able to tell us apart.

We are just standing here, one facing the other. (*Did I see him blink?*) Any movement seems absurd to me because, I accept it, it would be an admission of my madness. That is, if I lift my leg, it will only be to make sure this man identical to me is not really a man but a reflection—maybe even a man in a dream.

My subconscious tells me he may be my double, what the Germans tend to call a *Doppelgänger*. We all have a double, they say. So, what if he thinks this, too? Will he be afraid? Will he attack me? What does it all mean?

I don't know how many minutes have passed, but neither of us has moved. I think we have somehow gotten caught at an impossible standstill in the cracks of time and space. Could it be that this man is me just at the moment before I stood here? Am I his past self? Are we stuck and stranded in this plane knowing ourselves the same thing from different times? I reckon this might drive him crazy, my poor alternate I, thinking about this present that should have never been his. However, his face, like mine, only shows curiosity.

It's been too long now. This little conundrum has sucked my patience dry. But, wait, he moved! His right arm, he just moved it! Now he turns around... and I... Oh no! I'm not turning... I see him go, but I'm really not *seeing him* go, I only *sense* that he is leaving... I don't go anywhere... we are no longer face to face. And everything… very quietly, very faintly... has started to fade away...

Skeleton

The initial fright, quite brief, anticipated the rest of the story. Its effect must not be mitigated: although ephemeral, it was brutal while it lasted.

He woke up during the early morning, while still dark. He'd been doing that a lot lately. The prostate, his daughter had told him.

Before returning to the warmth of the comforter, he saw it. (Years later, when someone recognized him on the sidewalk and asked how things had transpired, he would reluctantly say, "It was a mixture of dread and surprise.")

There was the mirror, which was his size, and his darkened reflection, but, in the center, like an x-ray image, there was a skeleton. A suffused glow outlined its shape. He threw an expletive and slapped the air.

He looked around him. Nothing and no one in the room. Only the eerie snoring of his wife destroying the possibility of silence. The strange phosphorescent vision of the skeleton was still there, though, right next to his reflection. Fearfully, he reached out and placed his right hand an inch from the cold glass. He traced the outline of the spectrum with the tip of his finger, like a child in the grips of wonder.

With great curiosity, for a long while, he sat on the edge of the bed. The skeleton didn't seem particularly evil. In truth, it didn't seem particularly *anything*. It was just like any other hominid skeleton one sees in books or movies. As he stared at it, he thought of everything: the possible and the impossible—at some point, he even prayed. Then, he decided that his wife should see it, too. Be a witness. *Who will believe me if only I saw it?* He reasoned.

The instant he showed it to her, he felt an enormous blanket of remorse fall all over him. The woman screamed and jumped; she ran in her boring underwear straight outside and, from the garden, woke up the neighbors. She went back in and would not stop circling, pointing at the mirror, half-praying, half-cursing, and, somehow, blaming this entire madness (whatever this madness ultimately meant) on her mother-in-law.

She called her sons on the telephone and, in less than an hour, the house had become a sort of carnival: there were people crying, men taking pictures, children trying to touch the mirror, and drunks concocting theories. The nuns arrived, the neighbors with holy water and crosses, the Jehova's witnesses who lived in the brown-brick house, the prostitutes from the house on the east corner of the street, the carpenter... They organized themselves in the most regal manner and solemnly paraded in front of the mirror.

Some, as they walked past it, made the sign of the cross.

In no time, the authorities arrived, too. A man in a navy suit and wide tie asked him some questions and, without his consent, ordered the mirror taken away.

It took him two years to get it back. The morning he returned with it, hugged as if a lost pet, he thought of building a sort of altar where he could display it for a few bucks. He did this and, the truth is, the proceeds were barely enough to recover what he had invested in the altar and buy a can of coffee.

The scarce interest of the people surprised him. But, truth be told, he soon lost the desire to look at it, too. The luminous skeleton was still there, but the authorities had removed its mystery. They had done all sorts of possible studies and analysis without reaching a satisfactory conclusion. In time, they did what he'd feared they would do: they reduced the supernatural fact to a mere sensory activity. They, very publicly, assured this wasn't what it seemed—they laughed into the cameras reporting live. They said it was but a visual accident caused by the chemical composition of that particular mirror. "The only abnormal thing here, for sure, is the mirror's wrong molecular structure and its unusual ability to fragment light a certain way to create this optical illusion."

The fact that the skeleton never moved, talked or did anything at all didn't help, either. It was like a drawing, a big stain that had forced him to buy yet another mirror.

One afternoon, when he came home from the shop, he found the mirror in pieces. His wife shrugged and assured him it was better this way.

That same night, he felt someone leave the room. He opened his eyes with the expectation of, perhaps, finding the skeleton stabbing his wife dead with a sharpened tibia or, at the very least, strangling her with his bare bony hands... but he saw nothing. There was no one there.

He shook his head in dismaying disappointment, and, with a sigh, went back to sleep.

The plant in the rocking chair

The first time I saw her, I was on my way to my father's grocery store. This was about a year after the stroke that left mom with half her body paralyzed and an unintelligible mumbling—too sad to remember and too shocking to forget. In such unfortunate state, she couldn't do much. So, my old man was left without help and I, no other way around it, had to drop out of school to help him.

That day, to tell the truth, nothing seemed out of the ordinary about the woman. What caught my attention was how pretty she was. I was fifteen years old then and only cared to look at girls my age or so. But that woman was not like the other older women. Her hair was long and the color of cinnamon, her face had a delicate thinness to it, and her mouth was something you saw and craved, like the last sweet in the bakery display window.

She was sitting in a rocking chair, on a tiny porch that rose like a small wall from the sidewalk. A black iron fence imprisoned the porch, and more than once I imagined—seeing her always so alone, always in her own space—that the fence was a border separating her from the rest of the world.

As time went by, I noticed that the woman spent more and more hours in her rocking chair. I would see her early in the morning (Dad opened at five, just before daybreak, and I had to follow him an hour later), and again on my way back home. She was always at the same spot, with the same clothes and the same blank expression on her gaze, as if she hadn't moved to even drink coffee, eat or go to the bathroom.

It didn't take long before my curiosity grew. I remember asking Dad if he knew why that woman sat in her rocking chair all the time without talking to anyone. After a stern look and a brief lecture on minding my own business, he seemed to meditate for a few seconds and then told me that, ever since her husband, Pepe, whom people called *el brujo* (the witch man), and their two sons, Luis and Roberto, were killed in a motorcycle accident, Estela—that was the first time I heard her name—had never been the same.

I performed the same routine every day of my life until I was twenty years old—the routine of seeing, dreaming and desiring her. Mom had passed away two years earlier, and Dad and I decided to visit and bring her flowers that afternoon.

The cemetery was uncommonly full of people, I recall. At around a quarter past three, as Dad told a rigorously boring story about a friend of his at a different cemetery, I turned my head to the right and there she was. In front of her, there were three tombstones and a tiny statue of a little angel with a violin. That was the first time she ever looked at me. For an instant our eyes met and I could see the pain in her eyes was bigger than she was, probably the biggest thing she ever had; and her sadness consumed her inside out. And I saw something else in those eyes, something even deeper than sadness, which I could not then and cannot now put into words.

It was then that I finally understood what this poor woman had lost. My eyes watered up and Dad probably thought it was because of mom, for he put his hand on my shoulder and stopped telling that ridiculous story.

That was the first of only two times I ever saw her outside her home. From then on, everything was as before: on my way to the grocery store she was at her spot and all she did was gaze at the horizon. On more than one occasion, I wondered if she didn't work, what she ate, if some odd evening, God forbid, she'd thought about killing herself.

Dad died when I was forty. My twins, Bolívar and José, who'd just turned eight, behaved like two little gentlemen at the burial. Amanda, my wife, cried all the way to the cemetery and during our entire stay. As we were leaving, I had one of those inexplicable impulses and looked towards the grave of Estela's family. I felt a pinch in my heart when I saw her standing there again, with her unshakable sadness and her immense loneliness. Although I saw her every now and then in her porch, at that moment, standing there, her head downcast, I could appreciate the deterioration the years had burdened her body with: gray hair, drooping arms, withered skin… and that silence, that drowning silence which constantly enveloped her—as if she carried an invisible coffin on her back.

It was a Wednesday, I remember as if it were today, that I left the boys at the grocery store and practically jogged home to get some money for a small loan I'd promised Don Cucho. When I didn't see her in the rocking chair, it was as if pliers grabbed and twisted my guts. I looked all around me. People were on to their own businesses—no one had noticed Estela was not in her porch. I wondered how many, like me, saw her there and thought about her.

I took two more steps toward my destination, but stopped. Even before I made the first motion towards her house, I knew in the depths of my soul there was nothing in the world that could stop me. I had to make sure she was well.

I went up the three steps onto the porch. Not without embarrassment, I opened the door to the fence and noticed the entrance door to the living room was slightly open. With the three ounces of courage I was able to muster, from the threshold, I called her name twice. The silence that answered had the same voice as the silence that always surrounded her. Without further waste of time, I entered. I was not in the least surprised by the neglect I found in that house. Estela didn't have the mental presence for such things. I walked among broken cardboard boxes, paintings reclined on furniture, small tables with a random assortment of items, from shoes, flip-flops, and clothes, to hair blowers, hand towels and sleeping gowns... when I came to a corridor, that surely led to the alcoves, I saw a shelf and on it a few photos.

The deceased were there: smiling and full of life—in the almost cruel way photographs know how to appear to duplicate life. Their children were so young; and the man: he did not look the way I'd imagined.

An unexpected movement to my right startled me. I turned quickly (more violently than that slight shock warranted, surely) and saw a dark gray cat, quite eerie in its slow, lazy crawl, atop an armchair full of dust and time.

Ignoring the feline, I looked everywhere, all around me again, as if expecting to find some specific clue that would lead me exactly to where she was. And then I walked down the small hallway to the first room. The door was locked. I tried the one next to it, pushed the door open, and realized it was the children's bedroom. My skin crawled because I had the unmistakable feeling that I was being watched. When I turned around, the cat was there, his bottomless eyes fixed on me, as if studying me. But in truth my chill hadn't been just because of the strange cat, but because, now that I was a father, I empathized more deeply with Estela's tragedy. And when I entered the room, and thought about those two boys, I felt my heart shrink.

I took one last look in the bedroom and stepped out back to the hallway. In less than three minutes, I went through the whole house. Finally, I stood in front of the other room, the one with the locked door, and knocked. Nothing. I tried two, three times to no avail. With incomprehensible fear, I called her name. One, two, three times. Silence only and the purr of the damn cat, which only moved when I moved and in the same direction.

I was about to leave when it crossed my mind that maybe Estela was in the room and needed help. *What if she had a stroke or something?* I grabbed the knob, tried to figure where on the door I should hit, and lunged at it with my shoulder and with all my might. This room was empty, too. My next thought was that perhaps she'd gone to the cemetery again.

Something told me, however, this was not the case.

After a few minutes of meditation, I remembered Don Cucho's money, and told myself I'd done what I could. When I turned to go, on the desk, I saw a notebook. Now the truth is that it wasn't a notebook and I knew it: it was a journal. It was open and I couldn't contain my curiosity. Now, I would have given anything to not have read what I read.

In tremulous handwriting, written in obvious despair and with perhaps no presence of mind, the last entry read:

Forgive me forgive me my beautiful children I didnt know you'd go forgive me

I could feel sweat crawling on my neck. I looked around because (it is difficult to describe) the feeling that I was not alone did not go away. I felt that Estela was there with me. And this sensation made me perspire the kind of nervous sweat that's cold and plenty. I wiped it with my forearm and dared to turn a few pages of the journal. I read many fractions, several paragraphs, and even a poem Estela had written to her husband when she was barely fifteen years old. I closed it and reopened it, but now from the beginning. I read several pages. In them, Estela professed eternal love for him and overflowed with joy. I found blank pages, many, and some only had a few sentences, as if she'd wanted to write but could not find the words or the time.

At one point, something inside urged me to put down the journal and leave, but my curiosity was stronger. I read a few more pages and discovered that her husband had abused her. I felt anger. An illogical, inconsistent rage.

Estela confessed she no longer loved him, wrote she was still with him out of fear. More than once, Pepe had threatened to cut her throat, but not before killing the children. I don't know why my eyes clouded with tears. In a few moments, I was at the final entry again. Although I had no proof, it was logical to think Estela had done something to get rid of her husband, but everything had gone wrong.

What did she do? I kept wondering while snooping around every corner of that room. Sunk in restless thoughts, I stopped before a plant that rested on a rocking chair. It looked, at first, as any innocuous object looks, but then something caught my eye: The plant was not withered.

It did show signs that it'd been there for a long time. I found it weird that it rested on that rocking chair without a vase, without sand or water. I looked at it for a few minutes, scrutinized it, really. I even touched it, because it could have been an artificial plant, but no, it was a real plant and it was alive, despite having not a trace of flowers, leaves or anything. *This is the weirdest thing*, I thought.

The ringtone of my cell phone alarmed me. I still hadn't gotten used to the damn thing. I knew they said in a few years there would no longer be telephones in houses, and everyone would hang around with one of those incredible examples of human intellect. I didn't think so, but the truth was the damn little device was convenient.

"Hello? Yes, oh, sure, tell Don Cucho I'll be there in fifteen minutes. Tell'im to wait for me and offer him my apologies."

I flipped it closed, took one last look at the strange plant and the cat (which was once again staring at me and with no care to hide it), and made my way to the door. That's when I saw her. Even now, as I write this, my heart races.

Estela was reflected in the mirror.

She had the same blank stare as she always had, but this time around she was naked. Her wrinkled and aged skin seemed to have a kind of glow, a dull sort of glow, if such a thing exists, and in her right hand there was some sort of black amulet, with a feather and what seemed to me was a firefly, a fly, or some such insect. The whole thing made me sick and my heart beat faster.

I knew this could not be. Estela was not in the room.

With my heart threatening to throb out of my chest, I held on to the door frame because I felt I would, out of fear, drop down at any moment.

That's when I saw the detail, the horrifying detail: Estela's reflection was sitting in the rocking chair.

My whole body bristled, every single part of me. I turned my face towards the plant and then I saw it in its entirety, from the door, from that distance, one could tell:

Estela was the plant. The plant was Estela.

I ran outside, crossing myself a dozen times, vomiting... when I got to the grocery store, they had to call the doctor. They drove me to the hospital in an ambulance.

Sometime later, I learned that one of Pepe's sisters had dropped by the house and had everything relocated. Needless to say, I never told anyone a word about this. Neither did I ever see Estela again. In fact, when I could, I took the longest way to the grocery store in order to avoid passing by that house. One day, when my boys were of age and I was already an old man, it occurred to me to ask Papito, Blanca's son, how Estela's husband and children had died. He told me the matter had been kind of strange, because that man cared for nothing in this world as he did for that motorcycle. "That man took better care of his bike than he did his family," he said. "But that day, nobody knows what got into him. Pepe never took those boys out, ever. He was all about himself and his business. That morning, though, he got this idea: he wanted to bring the boys to the river to teach them to fish. And he did, quite early, but they did not get too far. The brakes gave out and they ran into a Trailer truck."

Today, on my seventy-eighth birthday, I've decided that Estela's story needed to be written, even if nobody reads or believes it, because strange things happen in this world and people hear about them, witness them even, but always remain silent.

I have concluded that Estela screwed up the brakes of the motorcycle in an attempt to get rid of her abusive husband, but fate dealt her a terrible hand. Although, perhaps, it was not fate at all. There may be a reason why she paid the way she did. After all, people always commented that this man was *brujo*, had dealings with the occult; and, supposedly, don't believe me, he even had a bacá[1] back in the house.

---

[1] **Bacá** is, in Dominican folklore, a demonic creature (which can take different animal forms) created through witchery, by making a pact with the devil to offer the owner's soul in exchange for protection and wealth.

The meteor

They announced it on Wednesday, August 7th, 2019. They said it during game time: Cleveland visited Milwaukee. Lebron vs. Towns.

I was on Instagram watching videos when the guy came up. What I remember best is the expression on his face—as if he had been forced to go on the air and say what he said. I can't say I remember the words. Those left my memory immediately. Only the news remained. To tell the truth, the news itself felt sort of detached. I kind of felt indifferent to it.

The guy said something like, "It's been confirmed. Unless a miracle happens and the meteor changes its course, in a month, it will crash into our planet... It'll... be the end."

And then he could say no more. I was in shock that this man had lost his composure in front of the cameras. Dude had been doing this job for so long, it felt like a betrayal almost. I spent more time recriminating his attitude than thinking about what he'd said. Then, with excruciating slowness, it dawned on me that the man, against his will and instinct, had agreed to go on the air perhaps for the last time. I think it was precisely at that moment the idea actually hit me: a meteor twice the size of the earth was on a collision course.

"...it's been confirmed..." I thought I heard the anchorman's voice once again.

This detail comes back to me now one more time: his eyes. They had a strange expression that, no matter how hard I've tried, I haven't been able to associate with fear, rather with something less mundane: the certainty that whatever amount of minutes he was spending in front of those cameras was wasted time. It did intrigue me how desperate he'd seemed; how bad he'd wanted to get it over with and just run away from those cameras.

On channel 64, a Hindu-looking lady gave details of the meteor threat with chilling coldness, as if, somehow, she had not yet understood she would not be able to escape the imminent clash, either.

At that precise moment my son video-called. "Hey," I said, smiling. "Pa', have you seen the news?" He asked me, his face pale and his hair a mess.

"Yes, I heard a giant piece of rock's coming towards us. Damn, how are we getting out of this one now, uh!" I laughed out loud as usual.

My son, on the other end, seemed quite serious, gloomy even. "What's the matter, boy? Are you Okay? Don't tell me you are fighting with La Martinita again."

"Bye, dad," he said, and then hung up.

I didn't have time to say goodbye or anything. His rudeness made me want to call him back and lecture him, the inconsiderate brat. We were about to die and all he could think of was being a worthless rebel.

At around 10:00 a.m., three weeks later, the meteor started to show in the sky. It was but a tiny dot of light that flashed intermittently and seemed really far away.

I was alone up on the rooftop, hung-over. We'd been a few days already with no electricity or telecommunication of any type. Across the street, the Curtis were in their backyard drinking whiskey and grilling steaks, pork chops, and hot-dogs. There were like seven of them. I would have liked a piece of roast beef, but forced myself to think of something else: that family, they weren't particularly clean, I'd been told. I could get salmonella or some shit like that.

That same week, on Saturday, I woke up from a long nap I had taken on the rooftop and was surprised to see the comet practically on top of us. It was a huge ball of fire and smoke that seemed not farther than the airspace altitude of commercial airplanes—I knew, of course, it was much, much farther.

At that moment, an overwhelming impulse entered my chest, an irrational urge to speak to some people I had not seen in a long time. And, also, a mighty desire to listen to songs from the 80s and to drink coffee, or something hot and sweet, like the chocolate in wide mugs grandma used to make. I couldn't tell why, but I also thought of my cousin Osvaldo, that old smart-ass, whom I never loved too well and whom I hadn't laid eyes on in at least twenty years.

Mind you, it didn't take long for these odd urges to disappear. What did last me a lot longer was the conviction that whatever was to happen ought to be rotund and definitive. I closed my eyes in an attempt to fall asleep for another little while, but, instead, meditated: *If we miraculously get out of this catastrophe alive, I'll sure be in a lot of trouble with the damn super of the building. I already spent the money for the rent, down to the last penny, on rum.*

That incredulous lot

Now the incredulous say the spinning sphere in the middle of the sky is not what I think. If it were, they say, there would be millions of videos out there just like mine. They demand that I stop trying to attract attention.

I've meant to tell them I have not made this up. The fact that this thing appears in my video can only be attributed to pure chance. My thing, you see, is to film birds. That's exactly what I was doing when I saw the luminous ball up above, spinning and moving left and right, and in all four cardinal points, like a restless child. Truth be told, honest to God, I didn't even pay attention to it until... well, until what happened.

The incredulous have come to my door. They throw trash and scream at the top of their lungs. I've meant to call the police, but ever since they started crowding in front of my residence, I've had no electricity or even a phone line. My old cell phone lies dead on the table and I have almost nothing left to eat.

I've decided, after so long, to go out and face them. Explain that, even if the video shows what it shows, it doesn't mean I support the others or anything of the sort.

It doesn't help, of course, the fact that lately I've grown scales on my skin, hooves on my feet, and my eyes have turned some odd shade of purple. I've given this matter some time to see if it'll go away, but I think I've got to resign myself by now.

As a matter of fact, out of sheer habit, I've even grown comfortable walking on all fours—as if I'd done it my entire life.

The aliens

The fact that they finally came was in itself the only remarkable aspect of it all.

The truth is we had imagined so many times, in so many ways and for so long, what it would be like to see them arrive that, when we actually saw the alien ship go through the clouds, engulfed in flames, as if just any other celestial body, and then crash into the ocean, it all seemed more like a poorly accomplished government stratagem than an invasion by technologically-advanced aliens.

Then, after several hours of tension, when the authorities grew tired of waiting—naturally worried—and decided to risk a team of brave individuals by sending them to perform the mandatory reconnaissance tour, we realized the aliens were not even remotely the superior (not even hostile) beings that for centuries we'd made them out to be; and who, in our minds, would come to attack us.

In fact, the authorities had to invest hours and personnel to rescue them. What we thought would be an alien invasion (with a certain morbid curiosity, I must add) turned out to be a space accident. It was never clear whether due to errors of the crew or mechanical malfunctions of the ship—which in its prime had been shaped like a long, pointy phallus.

The aliens were only three. Two were more or less tall in comparison to the third, who did not even reach the base of my tail.

Unsurprisingly, they were of a weird aspect: they all had four limbs. The upper two, they used frequently—and with some apparent urgency—to make countless movements while, with two shell-like protrusions on their faces, made unintelligible noises and sounds. The other two limbs, the bottom ones, they used to move around. It should be said that, although they were quite ugly, they were not the horrid, terrifying creatures we had for so long imagined they would be.

I remember, at the beginning, when we commented about them (since they had been recently found), there was a kind of collective dynamism, like hope, what do I know, that maybe we would learn things from them. But, over time, when the astonishment had passed—the novelty—and our scholars realized they were a rather primitive race (regardless of their surprise that the aliens had been able to develop technologies capable of interplanetary travel—or perhaps, that, too, was an accident), we all lost interest and returned to our routines.

Days ago, I passed by the zoo and saw them again. There are only two left: the tallest, whom we call just that, "the tallest", and the shorter one, which we call *Tokovy*, a meaningless locution, really, salvaged from a kind of inorganic material that covered him on the day of the rescue. Attached to this material, there was a smooth, rectangular object; and, on it, what looked like a kind of imprint (logically in the language of the aliens), whose meaning we could never decipher for sure, despite our data processors' conclusions that they were symbols akin to those of some of our various alphabets.

Someone suggested that *Tokovy* might be a name and, so, we used it.

The security guard at the zoo says they are hardly moving anymore. Something has happened to them. A scientist offered a theory of his (which we found extremely interesting) that had to do with *time*. "It seems to me that the aliens have brought time *within* their bodies. For some reason, their existence depends on it. I believe, as crazy as it may sound, that, as time moves on, it destroys them," he assured.

Today, watching the news, I've learned that the experts have been able to extract information from the machines they had managed to salvage from the wreckage. Surely nobody cares anymore, but they said it anyway: the aliens come from a small solar system with only eight planets, which revolve around a dwarf sun. Theirs is the third one closest to it and the only one that holds life.

That's it. I have given in to the idea that we will never know what they are really called or what actually brought them to our planet.

It saddens me to admit it, though, that they
are for the most part a disappointment.

The people in the mirror

The first time Niove saw them, she was five years old. They were in the mirror and their gazes seemed to have casually met hers. Mrs. Rebeca and Mr. Rufus, her parents, though dubitative, paid her due attention as she told them, and then proceeded to make the sign of the cross on her and on themselves.

The second time Niove saw them (curiously from the opposite mirror: the mirror in which they appeared was reflected in it), whether they realized she had seen them or not, Niove didn't know, because, when she turned around (afraid, yes, but determined to make eye contact), they had already disappeared.

This second time, however, the matter was much more serious, much darker. Niove, you see, was no longer a child. She was a fifteen-year-old bright young woman. Mrs. Rebeca had died five years earlier. Don

Rufus still dressed in black and cried when he thought no one saw him.

Niove got goosebumps more often than not. Even before seeing them again, she had always had the feeling that they were lurking—that inexplicable fear of knowing you're alone in the house. And yet, not quite. She had mentioned it to her mother; told her more than once, but Mrs. Rebeca didn't believe in those things. Or, if she believed, she didn't show it. On the contrary, she told her to forget about it, said they were childish nonsense, and it wasn't healthy to keep thinking about them.

Although she'd tried to forget it, Niove knew—she knew for sure—that it had not been a matter of the "reflection of the light", as her father had suggested, or "fear itself making you see things", as José, her best friend, had concluded categorically—as categorically as any fourteen-year-old might— right after she had told him she'd seen them.

Niove was convinced she had seen these people in the mirror. She knew she had.

In fact, a month before she turned ten, one of those afternoons when she felt she could do anything, she went to the mirror and, grabbing it by the bottom of the frame—with far more uneasiness than she'd ever experienced—using all her strength, she lifted it off the wall just an inch, and only for a few seconds. In that fleeting period of time, she had reckoned once she saw the wall—intact, normal—she would feel some relief. The truth was it made her fear even worse. Had she seen a hole on the wall, for example, a hole through which those people, by whatever incomprehensible means, managed to *appear* in the mirror and scare her, she would have been calmer, since that, although strange, would have been a somewhat more logical explanation. But, with no hole or entrance on the wall, they had no way to appear in the mirror—*What am I thinking?*—Then, the only thing left for her to think was that they were *inside* the mirror. And if they were, it meant this was, indeed, some sort of supernatural occurrence. From Lucifer himself, no less.

Niove was convinced these entities, who had also started to visit her in her nightmares—increasingly frequent lately and, to tell the truth, feeling as real as reality itself—couldn't be anything but dead people, or demons, who clearly wanted to harm her and her family.

Suddenly, still holding the heavy mirror, Niove felt—*I swear, mother, I swear to God!*—someone grabbed her hand. It felt as if a newborn were touching her fingers, but a newborn that had been resting in an ice pack or a deep freezer. The tiny fingers, like frozen ivy, slithered onto her skin and tangled themselves tight around her hand. She let go of the mirror and ran to her mother, crying hysterically. Mrs. Rebeca, with a confusing mixture of fear, doubt and pain (seeing her poor little daughter in such state), hugged her tight against her chest, all possible words stuck inside, like water behind a dam. Mrs. Rebeca kept glancing in the direction of the living room where the damned mirror hung. But all she could do was stroke her daughter's hair and whisper in her ear to calm down, to breathe, to pray... for everything would be alright.

A month later, a day before her birthday, Doña Rebeca was found dead. Niove was at school when Mr. Rufus found her lifeless body. Niove accepted what the doctors said, that it'd been a heart attack. A voice inside, however, told her something else had happened. That's why she questioned her father a thousand times about where, exactly, he had found her; what position she was in; what expression on her face... poor Mr. Rufus did not understand where so many questions came from. More than once, not to offend her, not to silence her with a slap, he strode away, eyes brimming with tears.

A few nights ago, she saw them again. There they were, the four of them, as if in a painting—one projected from the underworld.

It was a family: a man with sinister eyes, tall, and broad of shoulders. He was dressed in an ancient robe, centuries old, perhaps. At his right side, an expressionless woman, with a strange grin on her face, gave Niove the chills. And then there were those two children who, were it not for the darkness that resembled a black hole in the center of their eyes, could have passed for cherubs. And then, there was something else... something that looked quite familiar, which the woman held in her hand: her mother's favorite brooch.

They looked at her. All, at the same time, were looking straight and intently at her. Their ghastly gazes fixed on her face; and they seemed to smile the most sadist smiles, as if challenging her to do or say something.

Niove felt a sudden dizziness—as if pushed backward. She found her balance right away and looked at the odd mirror, but the specters were gone.

Without hesitation, she ran to her father's office. Mr. Rufus had his back to her, sitting at his desk, reading or contemplating something. Niove told him, as sudden as lightning, they ought to destroy the mirror in the main hall. She knew this mirror was one of Mr. Rufus's sacred possessions. He had inherited it, along with a golden tablecloth, some eggs decorated in fine linen and ivory, and a handful of extravagant feathers, along other things, from the Count, his father.

The treasures, as Mr. Rufus called them, had always been untouchable.

"I'm sorry, Niove… I'm… You know these things were inherited from my father. They are all I have of him."

Niove looked at him defiantly. "Dad, that mirror killed Mom," she told him, her voice firm, convinced.

Mr. Rufus shook his head and turned to the photo album he had been browsing when Niove interrupted him. It was a curt gesture intended to end the discussion. Niove took a deep breath and started to leave when, over her father's shoulder, something caught her eye. She walked briskly around him and then saw them: It was them. The people in the mirror were on the album.

Without a word, with both hands, she took the album from him. She stared at the photos for what seemed like an incalculable amount of time. And then she screamed.

She screamed and yelled like crazy, with tears in her eyes and a fear that, had it been liquid, would have flooded the entire house. It was them, she kept screaming, those cursed people had been stalking them from that mirror and now they'd killed her mother.

In a moment of fleeting insight, Niove stopped and turned to look at her father. That's when she saw it. Behind him, behind the desk, right in the center of the room, flanked by two huge bookcases: a mirror identical to the one in the living room opened there like a great gate.

Right at the center, like a king surrounded by his subjects, the Count stared at her sternly. The two children with demonic eyes and that lady with the aristocratic bearing and an unimaginably eerie smile stood by him stood by him. Now that they were so close, Niove realized they all bore a strange but clear resemblance to Mr. Rufus, as if they had, somehow, been the same person at some point, but time had worn away their features until they'd become less similar.

When she meant to react, when she came to, her father had already pierced her heart with a fine dagger decorated with a gold and ivory handle.

Slowly, gradually, she started to lose her vision, her sense of smell, her balance… and then, both pain and fear started to fade away, her consciousness...

Just before she glided completely into darkness, with a voice from beyond the grave, she heard the Count address the man she'd thought her loving father,

you are to find another family, dear one. Different town, preferably with no children...

Disappearing act

It had probably started long before I realized it was happening.

I was about to brush my teeth that night when I noticed a kind of stain, some sort of opacity on the mirror. Something minimal, which I would certainly have forgotten if, a week later, trying to remove an annoying long strand of hair from my nose, I hadn't seen it again. But there it was, in the same place and, perhaps, if my beautiful eyes did not deceive me, a little bigger. I mean, my reflection looked fuzzier.

I put my hand on the glass, sideways and in a fist, and tried to clean the mirror by making that circular motion one makes out of pure instinct. Nothing. There it was still.

It was then, at that instant, that I realized the strangest thing: the only blurry point on the flat surface was *my image*. Everything else was duplicated with the perfect fidelity we have grown to expect from mirrors.

My first reaction was, "What the fuck?!" Then, with painful slowness, the impression turned into unquiet and curious disbelief— the kind that keeps one awake till reckless hours.

The first thing I did the next morning, of course, was to look in the mirror. To my horror, there it was, my hazy reflection.

I had a vision at that moment: a giant hand was holding a yellow pencil—the kind that ends in a red eraser. It was the hand of God, which from top to bottom had engaged in the action of erasing me from existence. I almost shit myself out of fear.

Once again, like an idiot, I tried to clean the glass with my hand, even though, I already knew it was useless—something out of the ordinary was going on.

Then I thought, *maybe I should look at myself in a different mirror.* Not a step had I taken when a colossal fear stopped me: What would I do if this was real? What if in another mirror my reflection was also blurry? What the hell did this mean? Was I disappearing from the world?

Get a grip! I ordered myself. I knew I tend to lend myself to drama with annoying ease, so I shook my head with measured violence, trying to drive away those thoughts (had I been wearing a wig, it would have flown away). Walking with regal determination, I entered the room and turned on the light. I saw the fullness of my bedroom duplicated with impeccable exactitude in the wide mirror, but the space of my reflection; well, it looked thickly cloudy.

It came to me, just like that, the idea that I should react the way they do in movies: go crazy with frustration, scream like a mad diva, slam some shit against the mirror, scream some more... instead, I took a shower and went to my workplace.

On my way there, I was unable to avoid my blurry reflection. It was everywhere: in car windows, in rearview mirrors, in office glass doors, in every goddamn piece of glass...

I spent the day at work wondering what could be causing this phenomenon. And then, just when it was time to leave, in the elevator, I asked my friend Rachel the strangest thing: "Rachel, do you think everything appears normal about me today?" Stranger still was her response. Rachel looked at me and said, "Don't you worry. Everything will be alright." And her gaze, her eyes, were indecisive on whether to express sadness or disappointment.

I tried to ask her what she meant, but the elevator doors opened and people rushed in like cattle chased by rustlers and that was that.

That night, I went to sleep with a resolution: I would not look at the mirror. I did the same thing the next morning and, the rest of the day, which turned out to be my day off, I spent it avoiding my reflection. I was almost completely successful. That was until I succumbed to the temptation just before a date I'd planned with this stallion, Anthony, whom I had just met.

My reflection was even more diluted than before. And that terrible image of the gigantic hand erasing me with the pencil came back to assault me, like a bad omen.

I decided against going out. I didn't even call Anthony. I went straight to bed and thought about the whole macabre event of my progressive disappearance for at least three or four hours. The idea of consulting the all-knowing internet popped up in my brain and I searched for: 'reflection that vanishes'. I know it sounds stupid and useless, but what else could I do? As expected, a thousand articles and links appeared on the monitor, but none had anything to do with what was happening to me.

After sleeping quite poorly, the clarity of the morning woke me up. My body ached, as if I'd been beat up with a stick. For a minute there I had forgotten about the reflection issue. Weak of both spirit and flesh, I crawled into the bathroom, raised my face over the sink, and, as I turned the knob on the faucet, my gaze fell on the mirror. I might say the blur was still there, but that wouldn't do it justice. What I was witnessing was even more bizarre. Simply much more impossibly Dantesque:

My reflection was still blurry... but it had blurred into fucking transparency!

I could see the entire geography of the bathroom through my body!

It brought back to me the images of Sue Richards in the Fantastic Four comic books my brother and I used to collect.

Out of pure instinct, I touched my chest. Then I looked at my belly, my legs, my hands. Everything looked normal and in the right place; the only thing clearly not right was my damn mind. There was no mistake: my damn reflection was almost completely vanished.

I think *that* was the crucial moment, the exact instant of the loss of reason, the one step forth towards the precipice of madness.

I walked, no, I *jogged* in circles around the small apartment, thinking, thinking, thinking... At some point, I fell asleep. When I woke up, I was on my bed, cold, and my room was surrounded by a hundred, a thousand, a million mirrors. Tiny mirrors of all geometric shapes.

I think I slapped myself more than ten times. I felt like a stupid vampire who had just discovered the horror of mirrors: I no longer had a reflection. It was gone. I felt I was the ridiculous Nosferatu of a bad dream. This was a nightmare and I no longer doubted it.

I ran in my underwear down the hall. Down the stairs. Onto the street. I was screaming. And in the midst of my madness, I realized I had not seen a single person. There was no one around me. I was alone in the building, on the street, in the square... that's why I kept running with all my might and went to my work and saw the empty reception and entered the elevator—in my underwear and barefoot.

And in it, just as before, I ran into Rachel, my friend Rachel, and I almost hugged her. I say almost because, just as I motioned to do it, I saw that strange mixture of disappointment and sadness in her eyes again, or, was it perhaps... confusion and sadness, or, maybe, resignation and sadness?

And so, out of nowhere, she said to me one more time: "Don't you worry. Everything will be alright."

The strange window

The event of the strange window I'm going to tell you, even though it may seem crazy, actually happened to my dear friend Daniel de la Rosa, with whom I shared a large part of my youth in the neighborhood, and whom people nicknamed *Salami* (Dominican slang for lucky), because he slipped away from the clutches of death five or six times.

In a flash of lucidity, Daniel dropped out of high school to enlist in the military. It was more than evident Daniel was not about pencils and books. But he was willing to do everything else, especially take orders—besides, he was also quite the athlete. That's why we applauded his career choice and then saw him rise and progress, as far as circumstances would allow, in the military affairs.

All that, of course, until his athleticism betrayed him and he ended up sleeping with a lieutenant's wife.

He was dishonorably discharged and spent a year in prison for some crime we knew he had not committed. During that year, as if by magic, the saints, God himself, or the devil, in three occasions they tried to kill him, but the man, though badly wounded, survived.

I visited a few times and, I tell you, it was sad. But it was also something to behold, you know, how fucked-up, malnourished and turned-to-shit this man was, and still, from the moment he saw me, he would joke and laugh, and ask for the latest gossip, and laugh some more. Not a single complaint from his mouth, as if instead of a residence in hell, he was in a five-star resort.

The last time I saw him in there, I almost wept. I knew my good friend Salami would not get out of prison alive... and all that over some little pussy.

It turned out, however, that the evil lieutenant had a stroke on Christmas Eve and expedited himself out of existence.

Thanks to the efforts of some of his mother's friends (may her soul rest in peace), good old Salami got out in time to celebrate New Year's Eve. He looked like shit and hurt all over, but was alive and smiling.

What we didn't know was that the damn lieutenant was so petty, even after his death, he wanted to take revenge, and had commissioned his brother, a real bad motherfucker—a policeman people called *Colín* (the name of a double-edged machete)—that, if by any chance he died and Salami got out of prison, he was to avenge his honor.

And that's why Salami gifted himself a trip to Barahona, to a little town people called *Little Haiti*—go figure why.

It was here the story of the weird window took place.

A woman, whose name started with M, which Salami never learned to pronounce, rented him a room in a five-story building that worked as some sort of boarding house.

The room was at the end of a very long, dark corridor with no fewer than fifteen other rooms. Some had curtains for doors and Salami said those were the cheapest ones. Since he was a wanted man, he figured he would make an effort and rent one with an actual door and a latch to lock up from the inside.

Salami said the mysterious affair started the very first night. Said he fell asleep around nine thirty and felt as if he'd stepped into a lake of black oil. That's how dense his sleep felt, how dense and calm and deep. When he opened his eyes, thinking he would meet the brightness of day, he was surprised to see it was still dark. Even more so when he saw the time: a quarter past eleven.

He yawned, shook his head, and stood up to go pee. The boarding house had a single bathroom for every floor, way too far from his room. When he opened the door and saw the corridor in absolute blackness, he closed it back immediately and told himself he'd rather wet himself than step outside. He returned to bed and, just as he was about to collapse into the well of his sleep, noticed a slight clarity reflected in a small mirror on the opposite side of the bed.

He was instantly curious. First, because the truth is he hadn't noticed that mirror before. Second, because the reflected light seemed somewhat strange. It was a violet or purplish light, a single beam, which appeared to split the mirror in two.

He hesitated for a second about going to the intriguing light. His curiosity, though, was stronger than his reason. He walked and stood before it, scrutinizing it with avid eyes. The light was a blue-purple thin beam, indeed, which for some reason seemed to span only the space of the mirror. He turned to look behind him, towards the angle where, in his opinion, the source of the light should be. But there was only a wall there. No bulb, no candle, nothing coming from outside... It was at that precise moment Daniel realized the oddest thing: the room did not have a single window. It was a square construction of cement and blocks... with no windows.

He looked at the mirror again. As his eyes got used to the shadows, he gradually managed to discover his own reflection with increasing detail. But that line of light was still there, like a purple wound on the surface. *What the hell is this shit?*

He stood there for so long, trying to decipher this mystery, that, at one point, it was possible for him to distinguish almost all the objects in the room duplicated in the dark mirror. It also seemed to him, on a couple of occasions, that the light had flickered: "as if something interrupted it," Daniel said to himself in a whisper.

After a couple of hours, he got tired of it, went to bed, and fell asleep almost immediately. When he woke up, it was already noon. Around two o'clock, he showed up at a grocery store and asked the guy behind the counter if he knew where he could find Mr. Lora, a fat man who had a pawnshop. The guy looked at him suspiciously and gestured with his left hand that he didn't know.

Daniel thanked him and left. He leaned against the wall outside and waited for about half an hour. Two guys arrived in a Yamaha motorcycle and practically jumped on him, revolvers in hand. They forced him to get on the bike—right in the middle of the two, like a hot-dog sausage—and took him away without a word.

When they got to the pawnshop, and Mr. Lora saw him, they both laughed and hugged. "Damn, Salami, I thought you were some crazy asshole who wanted to do me. These fellas were ready to throw sand in your mouth, boy," he said, laughing. "I know, *manín*, that's why I just stood there, waiting."

Lora hugged him again and, after another glass of beer, asked him what he wanted.

"I do whatever it takes, *manín*, I just have to do some work until I can return to the capital," he said. "*Claro*, Salami, no problem, *tú eres de lo mío*. Beto, get Salami a gun and put him on the payroll. This is your house, *mi hijo*, you take it easy now." He gave Salami another hug, refilled his glass, and told him they would meet later.

When Beto returned, he handed Salami a pistol—*all rusty and shit*—put a hundred pesos in his hand, and told him to stay around and be alert. If he saw anyone weird hanging around, he was to shoot first and ask questions later… "unless it's the white dudes, you hear me? Those, you don't shoot."

That night, Salami fell asleep later than the night before. But, once again, he felt himself falling into an abyss, black, bottomless, stuffed with only one thing: silence.

He opened his eyes with the impression of having slept nine hours—when barely one had passed. And, again, in the mirror, there was that purple light that had no source. This time, for reasons he failed to associate with anything, he got scared. He looked around for he sensed he wasn't alone. *What is it with you, cocksucker? Since when are you such a cowardly bitch?* He scolded himself.

To regain some courage, he grabbed the gun and walked to the mirror. The violet wound split the dark glass in two. He looked behind him, like an idiot, to where he knew the light should come from. Then, out of sheer instinct, he put a finger on it. The shock made him gasp. He screamed a loud *coño*, and took two steps back. He pointed the gun at the mirror. The streak of light had grown wider. Not much, just a few inches, but it was definitely wider now. And he knew it had happened because he'd touched it. For a moment, he tried to remember if he had felt something, some strange sensation when he touched it, cold perhaps, or heat... but he concluded he'd not felt a thing.

After a few seconds, and still pointing the gun at the mirror, very slowly, almost shitting himself out of fear, he brought his finger to the light.

This time, he saw everything clearly: at the touch of his finger, what was a streak of light parted to become a luminous slit. Salami (whose testimony I still can't believe) inserted another finger, and then another, until he managed to widen the light as if ripping open a piece of cloth. Then, like someone looking out of a window, he saw into the other side.

The first thing he noticed was the intense clarity of the sun. So bright that for an instant his eyes were blinded. Then, adjusting his gaze, he saw a handful of people walking about. There was a man dressed in several layers of a fabric that seemed very fine, and women like those he'd seen in movies with their faces covered by a veil, showing only their eyes. There were baskets everywhere, tablecloths, food, vases, mice, pictures, lamps, rugs, and countless other things. Daniel squinted his eyes. With force, he squeezed them shut. When he opened them, the vision was still there.

He understood that, somehow, through that mirror, he had uncovered a window to another world, or to another place, to another country, what the hell, to another damn dimension...

A noise startled him and made him withdraw his hands. Immediately, the purple light resumed its linear shape and the mirror once again took over its space. Daniel saw the vague reflection of the things in the dark room, and his own face in shock and disbelief.

That night, of course, he could not bring himself to sleep. He got up a few times with the intention of seeing the vision again, but resisted the idea. As he meditated, it came to his mind this could be the work of the Haitians. He had heard it many times, that these people lived on voodoo and black magic; and thought—more like, convinced himself—that there was no other explanation.

Early in the morning, he showed up at the pawnshop and told Lora in great detail everything he'd seen. Beto was there, too, and a guy they called Pork Chop. They all looked at each other and, at the same time, burst out laughing.

Daniel got slightly upset but kept his cool. "*Compai*, you know I'm not one to make shit up. If you don't believe me, come see for yourselves," he said.

That night, Mrs. M felt like complaining when she saw these four men enter the boarding house as if they owned it, but when she saw it was Lora, she kept to herself.

Lora, Beto, Pork Chop and Salami stayed in the room for almost three hours. When the clock struck twelve, Lora got up from the bed, put his hand on Salami's shoulder, and told him to go to sleep, that it had all been a bad dream. Beto looked at Salami with anger and Pork Chop laughed at him, again.

Around two, Daniel heard a noise. He wanted to open his eyes but felt someone or something prevented it. He tried to speak, to scream, but it was as if he were inside a funnel, as if an invisible force covered his mouth and eyes. Within the fine border between dream and reality, as if through a mist, he saw silhouettes in the room. There were two or three; and he could have sworn one was a woman who moved stealthily. Then a blow to his head sent him emphatically to the other side of the border, to dream land, where consciousness has no will.

The sun slapped him warmly. He immediately looked in the mirror. Everything wore the stupid innocence things are disguised with during the day. He shook his head a couple of times to wake himself up. After a bath and a really tasteless breakfast, he spent the whole day running errands with Pork Chop and Beto. And then, at around seven o'clock that evening, he washed his armpits and balls; and went straight to a prostitution spot Beto had shown him. There, for about two hours, he fucked a brunette under twenty. Although she had only one good tit—the other one had a few ugly scars, he said—the hot young thing had *cocomordán*[2]: she squeezed his cock inside her like she wanted to yank it off and keep it.

When he fell asleep (almost as soon as he put his head on the pillow, which was hard as wood), he dreamed of the brunette with the scars. He was on top of her, once more enjoying in life the very glory promised (post-mortem) by any and all religions—connoisseurs as they are of the weaknesses of man. Yet in the sudden fashion of dreams, the brunette was no longer she, but

---

[2] **Cocomordán**: ability to exert considerable voluntary pressure on the male sexual apparatus (for pleasurable effects) during intercourse, through the pubococcygeus muscle.

the woman from the boarding house; and, standing behind Salami's back, there were four thugs with daggers.

Daniel woke up perspiring a soft, frozen sweat. Barely two seconds later, he saw the light. Determined, he ran to it and without hesitation put both hands on the luminous line. What he saw filled his body with electricity and goosebumps... and terror:

There were one hundred, nine thousand, twenty thousand burning men and women... there were dismembered children, old men covered in shit, pus, and blood… there were all kinds of people, of all races and sizes, and professions... and all their reeking filth sprouted from countless wounds they had all over their bodies. They were all naked. Everyone was screaming, yelling the most terrible curses Daniel had ever heard. Some saw him. They turned to him and tried to ask for help, but worms, flies, scorpions, shit and a pasty liquid came out of their mouths, as if their organs had been liquefied inside... and their eyes were indescribable, like dark stones the devil himself had violently rubbed one against the other a thousand times...

The scream he was about to unleash got stuck in his throat as powerful hands pulled him back.

He fell to the ground and saw four silhouettes. He knew these were the same people he'd seen the night before, in the kind of oneiric trance he'd experienced in the room.

He glanced at the table where the gun rested. He knew the table was in that direction but the truth was he couldn't see anything. Besides, it was too far, he knew. One of the men grabbed him by the back of his neck and brought a knife blade almost gently to his throat. The fact that he hadn't slit it yet made Daniel understand they weren't there to kill him.

They walked out of the room and on to the next one. There they made him wait for a long time until he heard a rooster crow twice.

That's when the woman came in. They forced him to drink some beverage she had brought in a plastic bottle and he felt like he'd spent hours fighting them.

But at nine o'clock in the morning, something happened. Something Daniel never recovered any memory of. All he recalled was that he opened his eyes and it was as if he'd dreamed the whole thing. The first thing he noticed was that the mirror was gone. He tried to remember whether or not this was the same room, but he couldn't say for sure. He looked around, searching for clues to what had happened. Without even brushing his teeth, he went out into the hall and found Mrs. M, who looked at him with the same equanimity as the first time.

Daniel was certain she was behind it all, of course.

He questioned her. She looked at him with devilish eyes and Daniel knew he'd been right—she was the woman in the room the night before. He took a step closer, as if to intimidate her, but three men emerged from one of the rooms, like hyenas. One of them hadn't even bothered to hide the knife. Daniel pulled out the gun and pointed it at them. But those men, the truth, did not seem to fear that object. "What's more," said Daniel, "it was as if they'd never seen a gun before, as if they didn't know or didn't care what it could do." Mrs. M spoke then, her voice raspy and unflinching, "Collect your things and go. Go away, right now."

Daniel went to Lora and explained what had happened. He put his right hand on Salami's shoulder and advised him not to mess with the Haitians. With that said, he poured him a glass of beer and urged him to make a toast. "For your return home, *mi hijo*. Just yesterday some *tígueres*[3] killed *Colín* in Capotillo. No wonder they call you Salami, *mi hijo*, you are the luckiest motherfucker I know."

I wish I could say Daniel went back and took it easy and got married and all that good stuff. But the truth is poor Daniel got a little bit crazier every day. And everyone noticed.

At first, it was only small stuff, nonsense: the accounts of the story of the window, the anecdotes from prison, things like that, which, from time to time, he would tell

---

[3] **Tíguere** refers to the street man, the thug, the conniving and wicked.

slightly differently. But then, we noticed he'd started to really lose the thread of the stories and, in a short time, he no longer said anything coherent. He said, for example, that in prison he'd met a man with a turban who gave him a golden pistol; that on Sundays a beautiful Haitian girl in her teens would visit him in prison and fuck him for free, just because. Also, that the window in the mirror looked into a place unknown to him then, but which he now knew clearly was the entrance to hell. And the men who worked for Mrs. M had cursed him because they found out the mirror was with him; for they'd spent their entire lives looking for it, never realizing it'd been so close to them all along. And now, Salami said, *he* was in hell, because, since that night, he had been dead, only nobody, not even he himself, had known it.

One night, at a moment when he seemed almost lucid, he told me, "I know no one believes me. I know they make fun of me, and think I'm crazy. I know it because I understand now what happened back then: I died and went to hell. *This* is hell. *My* hell.

The hell *I* must go through… because it's the one I always feared."

Mrs. Fate

At four o'clock in the afternoon, give or take a few minutes, I saw Mrs. Fate standing in a corner. We were by the train station. She was wearing a two-piece suit, round sunglasses and a matching scarf. She looked like any normal well-off person—maybe a little more striking but, definitely, less pretentious. She stared at me, as I did her, and when things got weird, without hesitation I approached her and asked if we knew each other from somewhere.

In a calm, ambiguous voice, she said, "yes and no," and smiled generously. "Would you like to know your future?" She asked me. "Do you read the Tarot?" "No, something better. I am in charge of your destiny. I'm a sort of contemporary *moirai*, or, to put it in simple modern English terms: I dictate your fate," she replied in an amused tone. "Well, I don't believe in fate, so..." I responded, already taking my first step. "To tell the truth, neither do I. That's why I'm here. It turns out, since the birth of the human kind, I have been acting in secret, spinning plots, directing steps, all in the shadows, see? But never, ever, until now, had it occurred to me that, if I am the one who controls the steps of man, then man is nothing but a puppet of mine. There is no free will. I have come to you to test this theory. What do you think?" "Well, it seems absurd to me, really. Let's say, however, that I play along. Why did you choose *me*?"

Mrs. Fate looked around. She pointed at a woman. "It could have been her or that gentleman in the red beret, even that child. But, things of fate (she smiled), you are the chosen one," she said. "Randomly, then," I said. "Randomly," she replied.

It was my turn to look around. Life went on as usual. As a matter of fact, I was surprised by the brief doubt in my chest of whether or not the encounter with this strange woman was indeed some supernatural occurrence.

"What do you say then? Shall we try?" "What are we supposed to do?" I asked.

Again, that plain, unassuming smile. "I am going to write something on this piece of paper. I am going to give it to you and you will keep it without reading it. I will take my leave and, if you make your own decisions, we will soon meet again. If, on the other hand, things are as I suspect, that you have no say in your destiny, then we will never see one other again."

For a few seconds it seemed to me there was only the echo of her voice in the universe repeating those final words.

"That's it?"
"That's all."
"I agree, then."

Mrs. Fate wrote something on a piece of paper, handed it to me and, making a cordial gesture of farewell, took several steps towards the station. I was left with a terrible feeling: if I let her go without the conviction that all this was real, I would never be able to explain this conversation to myself. I would not even know whether this was a dream or an episode of schizophrenia.

"Wait," I almost yelled, "what if I read the paper before you leave?"

She turned around and, for the most fleeting of instants, a thin veil of sadness appeared to cover her face. Without a word, she kept walking.

When I got home, I took the paper out of my pocket. It read: "If you ask me for permission to read the paper, then you are not the master of your destiny."

I've never seen her again.

Alam Etreus A.K.A. The Greek

His name was Alam Etreus. Mom told me he was Greek. "The most handsome man to ever put soles in this town," she confessed, sigh and all. She said that, as soon as he arrived, barely out of his twenty-fourth birthday, with a body just like Kaliman's and fiercely sweet eyes, two things happened which few men in town appreciated: all the girls (and the married ladies) fell in love with him and he set up a store where he'd sell rugs, lamps, vases, and countless trinkets that soon sold like freshly baked bread. Mom said, "because, the truth must be said. It was more erotic to talk to Alam Etreus for five minutes than to sleep with our brutes our entire lives."

Needless to say, the poor Greek made more than one enemy. And even though he was not even remotely the celibate good shepherd he professed (at least one divorced woman and another one from the sinful yet joyful life of paid pleasures gave faith and testimony of the virtues of the good Greek), no one ever heard of any punishable misconduct, say, with some of the damsels of marriageable age or ladies with children, monotony, and husbands too busy to remind them that, apart from being housewives, they were also women. "And for the record," Mom said, "he had plenty of offers."

But jealousy is like rice: it grows when heated and the more water you add, the mushier it gets. Therefore, the men began to stalk (and curse at and plot against) the poor Greek. In fact, more than one, drunk, forgot the man was over six feet tall and threw fifty-pound bags over each one of his shoulders with the same ease he held a flower to gift one of his many admirers. Those who forgot and launched—like David against Goliath—an attack at good old Alam, woke up with a black eye or with the taste of their own blood in their lips. Alam would greet them after, as if nothing had happened.

"The truth is he was a good man. That's why what they did to him made us so sad," said the old woman, with true sentiment.

"One afternoon, don Vicario, the meanest man we ever met, showed up at Alam's shop and asked him for some rugs. These were in the back (whoever had visited the store before knew this clearly), which gave Junín and Calvario enough time to hide the object endowed with the witchcraft in the bottom of a box full of random stuff. We didn't find out about this until some fifteen years later, when, on his deathbed, Vicario confessed to Father Lucio, so he would not go away with that terrible sin. The rest is of public knowledge, son," Mom continued, "that same night, good old Etreum's tent went up in flames. No matter how much he thought about it and inquired, he never found the reason for the fire. Just like that, he went from his good life to destitution.

Since only the men had businesses, no one gave him a job. Some of us managed to pass him food a few times, but that didn't last. During the day, he wandered around, downcast, and at night all he did was stare at the stars. A month later, with a small bundle on his shoulder, he left town. He was already skinny, and his beard was no longer the handsome thing it used to be, but a dirty, ugly tangle. Two weeks later, news came that he'd been mistaken for a thief who'd been terrorizing another town and they beat him with clubs. Then, perhaps looking for luck, he tried to stow away on a locomotive but was so weak he lost his balance... and a hand. A year later, we learned that, in the town of Martalá, there was a one-armed Greek who roamed the streets telling jokes and stories to earn a piece of bread. Two years after that, he was arrested for stealing a chicken and there he remained for five hundred days. In Dubalié, he lost an eye. In Maqui-tlán, they kicked him out of the Church. In Visuní, they said he was a heretic, lashed him a hundred times, and then poured vinegar and salt on his wounds. In the city of Mustiná, he was declared insane and spent a year in a mad house.

On his last night on earth, Alam asked Allah why he'd faced such misfortune. And Allah's response was to restore his memory of the day he'd been cursed. Alam nodded, having understood everything.

Believing this understanding would some-how free him from the dark sorcery, he got up–with impetus he hadn't had in decades–and reached a small brook, where he washed his face and, with the edge of a stone, removed as much beard as he could. When he recognized his own face in the mirror of the water, he remembered that slight gesture: a smile. In his mind, in his heart, something told him his years of bad luck were over; from that moment on, he would resume his path. He became convinced that he should go to town and find work. He looked up at the sky and once again asked Allah to enlighten him, to send him a sign.

Determined, he took a first step. His right foot tripped over some metallic object: It was a lamp. He looked at it with utmost curiosity. His faith was so great he hugged and kissed the lamp, and whispered into the air it was time to rebuild his life. Like a child, he thought of rubbing it and smiled again.

He had not advanced a hundred feet when they found him with the lamp in his one hand. There were five. He only understood the word *thief* before they came at him with daggers and axes. In a matter of minutes, Alam Etreum had his single eye fixed on a point beyond the clouds and the stars. The lamp an inch from his severed fingers.

The book

On the all-too-normal night of the writer's death, they found *The Book* half open on his lap, a tall glass of *Concha y Toro* reserve of '86, half empty, and the gun on the waxed, wooden floor of his tiny apartment strategically located on Koellnerhoffgasse St.

If one were to say it in a single sentence, it would go something like: "His last book killed the writer." Depending on the journalist, there would be syntactic variants, but it would be more or less the same: "The writer was killed by his last book" or "Book kills writer." Of course, a sentence is not enough to explain what took place. It is necessary to elaborate. To say, for example, that the writer enjoyed a certain popularity and trajectory, that his colleagues respected him for both his work and his age (he was already past 70), that he was frequently invited to events and presentations, and his penultimate book, *The Naked Fly*, had been a modest bestseller. It also seems prudent to point out that he was highly regarded by his publisher and plans of expansion had already been put in place.

Logical to think then that the writer was in a position to feel comfortable with himself and his work. This idea was decisively outdated when, that night of unremarkable normality, the writer took the revolver and blew his brains out.

It is curious how an action so trivial and mechanical, such as the pulling of a trigger, may be capable of irremediably altering the ordinariness of the night already mentioned, say, for example, in the priest's house (the third one from the corner) and in the next one, where a widow with an unpronounceable name dwells: both suffered the shock of the thunderous shot.

Figuratively, the book pulled the trigger.

The idea is not unreasonable if one takes into account the last conversation between the writer and his editor, a short German man of those who, in conversation, nod with great vigor and say very little. It was he who made the compact headline possible: he asserted the writer had confessed to him, while pondering the possibility of translating *The Book*, the following: "If a ten were required to indicate perfection, for reasons of modesty, I would grant this book a nine. But, in truth, this is *The Book*."

But *The Book* arrived, made a few rounds and, unfortunately, without commotion or glory, passed.

The perfect book, the spoiled book, did not even deserve a favorable or negative comment from among those closest to him. Whenever they inched close to the subject of his work, they exclusively spoke about *The Naked Fly*—with growing bombast. He noticed, with increasing anger, that this book was now being flattered more intensely—he deduced they were doing it out of pity. There was not a single newspaper or magazine that dedicated an article, even a paragraph or a mention to it. Outside of the first two weeks since its launch, no bookstore reported sales. The editor tried to soothe him. Told him the critics of the masterpiece *The Book* clearly was would soon realize the mistake they'd made; told him not to worry anymore and, to comfort him, informed him that important people had shown interest in *The Naked Fly*—and there was even "word" of perhaps making it into a film.

In the writer's mind, however, it was inconceivable that no one could see the greatness of those stories, the hidden messages, the undeniable grace of the prose, the almost unprecedented beauty of that vocabulary...

It was just then, while sipping the wine, that he conceived the irrefutable idea. He didn't entertain it for longer than a minute or two. The author got up, took the revolver and shot himself dead.

Literary utopia of a vengeance

In 1966, on my first trip to Mexico, sitting in a curious Café with a pink corner, I met a nonagenarian by the name of Pedro Vicario.

The old man told me, with less mystery than I would have imagined the news warranted, that two brothers were looking for him to avenge a murder he'd committed decades before, and, being so old, he had no way to escape.

We had coffee together. I, of course, had not believed a word he'd said, but found it unbecoming to say so. At that, a woman with more miles than years in the journey of life arrived and greeted him effusively. She had been dazzling in her youth, it was obvious. Some tough man had surely killed for her if she ever asked.

"Dear, I am very sorry about Sierva María," the old man told her. The woman nodded, glanced at me without interest or manners, and went on her way. Mr. Vicario—with a wicked grin—told me she was *La Lujanera*—as if the name ought to mean something to me.

Noticing that he seemed a little anxious, I asked him if perhaps he wanted me to accompany him somewhere.

The old man shook his head, covered in a white tangle of fine, shiny hair. Between his teeth, he said something: mentioned a certain Juan Preciado, who had arranged to meet him at this Café to tell him about a ghost town. "I don't believe in those things," he clarified, "but I know a gringo who pays up to two dollars for stories like that. It's too bad Juan's running late. Any minute now, surely, he will not find me."

The Café, perhaps it's worth mentioning, was located at the train station. I was waiting for the train. My visit to Mexico City was a professional matter. I was investigating the death of a friend's great grandmother. Juliana Burgos was her name. She'd been killed a hundred years before in Turdera by two brothers nobody seemed to remember anymore. They killed her out of jealousy of one another. These events took place in Argentina, but my investigations had led me here, from where I'd make the long train journey to a town called Macondo, where the red-haired, soulless brothers had been seen last.

After a short while, two men stopped in front of Mr. Vicario. One, the slimmer, drew a dagger. The other one, equanimous, said out loud, "Don Pedro, we have come to avenge the unjust death of our uncle Santiago Nasar. We have told everyone in town, but, you see, history repeats itself: no one has come to prevent it."

The old man took but a single glance at them. He then nodded, put his hands on the table, and, solemnly, looked at me.

Then, they killed him.

Don Adudal learns Stephen Hawking has died

I just heard that a man died. They said he was a good man, who had accumulated a lot of information in his head and left some interesting advices and riddles. I hear people are surprised at the death of this man. They tell me he spent years defying death. But someone said it was strange that he died and I thought this an exaggeration. It doesn't seem weird to me. Does it seem strange to you? That a man, or two, have died, or a woman or a child? That shouldn't seem strange to anyone. Sad it must be, of course, as every death must be cause for sadness, sure, but there's no surprise, there's nothing unusual about it. The strange thing would be, for example, to hear there's a man who hasn't died yet. A truly old man, let's say. Or maybe a goat that has been alive since before the good lamb that took away or tried to take away the sin of the world. That, don't you think, would be really strange. It would be quite strange, I say. A goat that's two thousand, maybe three thousand years old, and still eating grass and jumping over little mounds of shit.

But the fact that a man has died, a man who was big and deep like the universe, a man who had no trust in lambs or man's fantastic elucubrations, well, that is something else, and it is not astounding. One is saddened, of course, that men die, that girls die so untimely, that poets and the children of merchants die, but grief, you see, has nothing to do with the fact that people know how to die. After all, and I know you will agree, are not we all immortal until the moment we pass?

Because, think about it, how do we take the mantle of immortality from someone who has not yet died? That would be pretty strange, right? Just like it would be pretty weird also to know for sure such-and-such cannot die.

Ah, *that* is news. But we are so mean, humans, listen, the very next day, what do I say, the very same day of this announcement, one, or two, or three, goes to the presumed immortal and shoots them. Because, it's sad, it's so petty, I tell you, human vanity and incredulity. If you hear a man has died, what can you do? Well, go on working, brother, go on eating rice and beans. Because there's nothing you can do.

It doesn't matter much when it's your turn to die if you're a genius, if you scan the cosmos, whether or not you leave behind a fervent legacy of theories, questions and answers. Those things are useless when a man dies because death is not a rare thing. If you ask me, I would tell you, what does matter is the other thing, the opposite: having lived. If there were joys, if goals were achieved, if you loved and were loved. See? In short, the dead is rarer than death itself. You get that? What they thought and said and did remains, but he or she doesn't. That which produced what was thought, what was said or done, that which occupied the now unmoving body, the hard puppet, is no longer. That is really weird. Think about it: when you see a woman, sleeping or standing, you know that sooner or later she is going to move, laugh or get scared. But the dead, genius or neophyte, what they lose is the world.

Dying should be but a simple event: a blackout, a reset. The dead person *is* the rare thing: he or she loses the absolute and does not realize it. Or they lose the past in the superposition of another present... and do not experience it.

Then we are left with what is truly strange: this foreign body already devoid of adverbs. Do you see it? It is now impossible to *adverbiate* the dead. To *adjectivate* it, sure thing, because from the moment death touches it, it is a name, a proper noun, an object. But not just *any* object, no: it is a grave object, a degraded object because it has lost the only thing that differentiated it from the other objects, from men and animals in the world: its memory. Can you see how rare the dead man is? How sad it is to go from man to dead man?

Some people, more practical perhaps, would say death is nothing more than the transition from person to thing. *The rite of inanity.* It sounds poetic, but it's pretty weird. And it's pretty real, too. Not death itself: dying is the most common thing in the world. What is rare is this objectivation of the body.

In fact, see, the dead body even limits *us*. From its own limitation, it limits us. Because we can no longer say it does anything. And *that* is weird. We could say this ability to make us cry and to limit us are the only possible things that can come from that body touched by death. That is to say: observe this body, which a while ago—and who knows for how many years—moved, screamed, and laughed at any bullshit, and realize now we cannot say it will "any moment now" stand up and tell us a string of stupid things from the hereafter or from the thereafter. Just imagine contemplating that thing with arms, eyes, fingers and ears, contemplating it for a long time, for a very long time, and never, ever again be able to say: *look! it has moved*, or, *its eyes are moving*, or, *see, the bastard has raised his voice*. That's weird, really weird and terrible.

Ah, the things those who die do to us, the living. They go to who-knows-where and leave us with the sadness of the unknown, with the mystery of a body without motion or senses, and with the certainty that, wise man, atheist or believer, death moves us away from this chubby or real sexy body— which one has used for so damn long that, good or bad, one has even grown used to and learned to like.

The rope of discord

When I did not find my rope, I knew, right away, that my neighbor (and sworn enemy), Abraham Vistolam Huerte, had stolen it.

I got hold of a log of wood (four feet long by half a foot wide, square of shape, which I used to secure the thin door of my little apartment) and without much thought I went out to find him. With each step, both my anger and conviction grew. I remembered, like someone who forcibly sees a retelling of his own story as a summary/documentary, each of the grievances the son-of-a-bitch had caused me: from the fifteen minutes I had to spend under a downpour because that animal had locked the entrance door—as if he were the only resident of the building—through the shame he made me suffer in front of Doña Nona (I still cannot understand how I allowed myself to be fooled into recommending him, knowing the rat Abraham is) when she asked for a candid hand to help her with the plumbing and this piece of crap with eyes offered his services—not knowing the first thing about plumbing—; to the mess he got me in with Chavela, when he told her (it was he, who else hates me?) she was not the only one I'd put my aim on—even told her I'd already screwed Miguela and Mecho.

By the time I stood outside Abraham's little door, decorated with a hand-drawn sign that read: 'Fuck outta here', all these memories had already convinced me he'd stolen my rope; and I swore right then and there this would be his last affront. I gripped the log with all my might and knocked on the damn door three times. The waiting and the anger brought me back the afternoon of the fist-fight. I felt my anger increase rapidly. I knocked five more times and then called out my enemy's name with as many decibels as my lungs would allow.

But my memory had already dislodged the way bad memories know how to do.

I saw myself drunk in front of both Negro's grocery store and Abraham—with his lizard eyes and his raven or hyena laugh, skinny as a syringe and devilishly sarcastic. The other men also made fun of my drunkenness, but it was he (who hates me the most?) who'd started it all. That's why I went on to him. But I had drunk so much rum that, before I could hit him, I lost my balance and ended up making a full turn on the axis of my own drunkenness, falling face down on the unpaved street. I got up, all dusty and with an embarrassment the size of the town and its history, and launched my next attack. This time I did not even get to attempt the blow: Abraham's fist, which was so bony it could have passed for a knife, stopped me cold when it came in contact with my face. That single blow was enough to momentarily banish me from reality.

Now the reality was Abraham had stolen my rope and, since he would not answer, even though the radio was on inside the apartment, I had no choice but to break down the door.

From thought to action, it did not take a second. The door collapsed with the docility of a feather and I stormed like a madman into that tiny, dirty room. Right in the center, like a flaccid tie blown by a powerful wind, Abraham Vistolam Huerte, the only man I've ever hated in my entire life, hung from a beam. Tied to his neck, my rope.

An indescribable sensation of satisfaction warmed me inside as I confirmed my suspicions of the theft.

The very skinny man, with a decidedly purple face at that moment, moved (surely without wanting to) in the style of worms, to the dizzying rhythm of death.

I looked at him for a long time. Curiously, I no longer thought or remembered any of the things that had tormented me before. My world had been reduced to this instant of quiet waiting and the equanimous feeling of knowing the worst was over.

Later, when I considered that this body, once my enemy's, would no longer move, I took the nearest chair, got on it, and, with a little dagger I always carry on my belt, cut the taut rope.

Claustrophobia

Two days after his burial, Amlale Walker opened his eyes. Thus, the intimate prophecy of his deepest fear was fulfilled.

It is necessary to specify that the expression "opened his eyes" is not exactly what happened. Amlale opened his *sight* from absolute sleep to timeless wakefulness. That is to say, the good man was dead—he, his family, and friends had already accepted that fact. However, he, not his already inert body entrusted to the soft earth, to the roots and to the eager maggots, but *he*, what had led that body, was not dead.

That was the horror.

Ever since he learned of his illness (when he was still enjoying life with the fullness of one who does not suspect his end as close as his shadow), when he learned of the inexorable advance of death inch by inch, organ by organ, like an army of cruel conquerors, he had accepted the inevitability of his impending demise with great stoicism. He had no choice. Crying, pitying, hating the world... what use would it all be? Death neither sees nor hears.

So, from the moment the doctor broke the news, Amlale weighed the fact with the same calculated objectivity he accorded to everything else. That night, alone in his room, he did cry for half an hour, but that was it. The next day, he did not shed a tear or the day after, and, after a week, it was as if the doctor hadn't told him he had, at the most and with some luck, two months left to live.

That weekend, taking advantage of the fact that the whole family gathered at his sister Annette's house every Sunday, after lunch, when most of them were resting in the living room, Amlale gave them the blow of his news without fuss or drama. He would never understand why, from that moment on, from the instant he saw his relatives cry their lungs out, he started to feel fear.

That's why it seemed like a favor of fate that the good doctor had erred in his prognosis and, already by the fourth week, he woke up on a Tuesday with excruciating pain... and begging to be shot in the temple.

They took him to the clinic. Sedated him. They accommodated him as best they could. On the third night, he passed away.

It must be said that, two nights before his death, another fear, conceived during sleep, wedged itself in his head and, like a thorn in his foot, would not let him die in peace. On the mural of his mind, he saw a question: what if you wake up after being buried?

He literally opened his eyes and found the ceiling of the room a few feet above his face. His first thought was that, in the coffin, he would not enjoy such distance. *It will only be two or three inches*, he thought, and felt a shiver run through his anatomy. Such was the fright, that his heart fluttered; and his sister, half asleep in a chair, got startled and, with a jump, came to his side. She then saw the terrible fear in his eyes. Shock and helpless-ness so great, she fell to her knees and began to weep.

After a while, he succumbed once more to the powerful embrace of the sedatives and, again, as if an enemy on the prowl, that horrible question returned.

This is how he spent his final hours: fearing, not death, but claustrophobia. For dying, it had been his all-time belief, was nothing but a disconnection, the inexorable unplugging from existence. He had never believed in absurd promises of a beyond, of eternal life, ghosts, nirvanas, or harems with virgins waiting for his virtues. Death would be literally closing your eyes to sleep until becoming completely unconscious. That was why he'd made peace from a very young age with the fact of ceasing: because it was inevitable and because it promised him no other quality than nothingness. He had lived his meager forty years with this strong conviction. If ever for a moment he'd doubted or feared, it was enough to remind himself of the inevitability of death to drive away his dread, to resume his cheerful living, his slight hedonism, and his vain journey without major worries.

But now, in bed, in death, his mind betrayed him. Existence itself betrayed him. How was he capable of thought while dead? Death had come to him and now he thought he would have liked to die as a hero of himself, just as he'd lived: carefree (charlatan, even), devoid of prejudices and fears, oblivious to complications and dramas. Anyway, was it too much to ask to die as one had lived? Yet now, lying there, self-conscious, and experiencing an even greater fear than the devastating apprehension prior to his death, he encountered grief, anger, shame, and bewilderment in knowing he had died under those circumstances: he had died a coward.

Of course, it was worse now, wasn't it? Now he lay just four inches from the end of his wooden world. His irrational fear had come true and here he was. Although he knew his eyes weren't open (perhaps in an instinctive manner he understood that he "saw" without actually looking); and although he knew this unbearable sensation of suffocation could not be real because, well, he was already dead, he did not stop experiencing these things with the same sharpness and even naturalness as in life.

Here was the coffin. He was inside.

He fixed his gaze on the mortifying proximity of the lid, noticed the bone-white color of the padding material, the patterns in the design, the lines and the obviously intricate details invested in every little thing, and wondered if perhaps these bastards knew something; something neither priests nor teachers nor philosophers knew, because, why bother with so much detail if no one would see them from the inside? He felt himself shudder. With sudden violence a blaze of great anger ran through his body.

It only lasted a second. Longer was the foolish feeling that his lungs were still struggling to process the oxygen they couldn't breathe. This caused him an illogical sadness, this and his body, because he felt it somehow, just not like before. He felt the terrible immobility of his body as if it were an extension of the coffin itself, made of cold hard cedar... and lifeless.

The next horror did hit him hard: he tried to close his eyes but couldn't. He had no eyelids in his abstract death situation. He felt he was at the epicenter of an irrationally cruel nightmare. But a nightmare dreamed by others, an invention of torture without time or space. With excruciating thoroughness, he knew this was the worst thing that could happen to human beings. But *what* was this? Right then, he conceived the intractable speculation: *Have we, in our infinite ignorance, buried and burned our dead forever and ever without knowing (oh, the horror!) they were still conscious inside their bodies?*

He screamed.

It was the most powerful scream ever produced. But he was dead. Decidedly dead. The scream took place only within himself. Without sound. He thought, *millions and millions of women and men and old people and children (children!) under the earth for thousands and thousands of years, suffering the direst punishment of ignorance. Thousands of years, all eternity, watching it go by, unable to close their eyes, unable to move, unable to go anywhere, gazing only at their increasingly rotting wooden coffins, prisoners of the earth.*

This had to be a ghoulish nightmare, indeed. Whose depraved mind had conceived such atrocity, such torture?

No, this could not be. So much cruelty was not possible. When did the *I* die then? When and how? He thought bitterly of his grand-parents, his parents, his poor Aunt Alicia... suffering all these decades under the dark earth. *Rest in peace*, we told them, *rest in peace. It's a joke!* He screamed again, once, twice, ten times, his atrocious screams without sound, and tried to put his hands to his face in an attempt to emulate the useless me-chanical gestures he made in life, but there, under the damp earth, with the almost plea-sant smell of mud, limited as never before by the still-scented cedar, none of this was possible. The only thing left was to see, suf-fer, think... and smell?

He smelled!

Yes, he could smell. He smelled everything, from the indistinguishable aroma of mud, to the freshness of grass and roots, to the scat-tered but sweet scent of the tapestry of his new home. The smell of the vast and deep earth around him. How was it possible? How was any sensory experience possible through a body that no longer worked?

There was no time to reply. Terror returned to shake him: he would smell his own rot. He would smell the progressive deterioration of his skin, he would smell the disgusting worms, the pus, his rancid blood, the stale feces... This couldn't be. It was unnatural, illogical, crazy.

How could so many centuries go by without anyone noticing the dead have not really stopped seeing and thinking? What actions then are we to take with the deceased?

He thought that maybe there should be no such action.

Man is matter and energy. Perhaps the earth and the universe claim them at death; perhaps they require direct contact of the defeated body with the earth, air, sun, rain...

And then it hit him: *It's the coffin! The damned man-made wooden prison! In our aesthetic desire, in our religious stupidity, we have been interfering with the natural process of death. We've condemned all of our beloved to eternal confinement. To the fire! We have turned their bodies to ashes and, oh no, have we entirely truncated their true end?*

There the suffocation returned. Uncertainty. The feeling of infinite regret threatened to sink him further into the earth, as if it could perhaps push him to break through the bottom of the coffin and drag him to the very center of the planet.

Right away, like everything that took place down there (he realized everything happened without succession, one thing over the other, in a kind of bracket where time neither chronology nor before nor after existed, a kind of constant déjà vu), the vision of the center of the earth gave him back that other vision in an encyclopedia with a red cover and gold letters, and he saw himself a child opening that beautiful tome (it was as if he could feel the weight of the book in his hands, the light dust, the singular aroma of those glistening pages), and felt again the wonder and amazement of seeing for the first time the majestic photographs and illustrations: a Bengal tiger, a telescope, an iceberg, the deep purple bougainvillea, a book of Wells... and then he saw it. And when he saw it, when he understood, when he felt the thrust of a fear even more overwhelming than all his previous fears together, he wanted to close his lidless eyes, wishing with a will not even in life he'd possessed to be able to unsee what he had seen, to return to the images of the tiger, the Colossus of Rhodes, a pretty Ethiopian woman with her breasts exposed and happy...

But he already knew with fatal certainty that, what has been once seen, is inescapable. Abandoning himself to the sincerest crying, he recovered the last image, the one he should not have seen, the one that made him understand and finally accept the reality of his sad circumstance: a drawing of hell.

135

On a fine morning, like any other, Mister Lleweraf did not wake up nor did he ever realize he hadn't.

Edgar Smith, Villa Consuelo, Dominican Republic. Writer, editor and translator. He has published over a dozen books, including **Gnuj & Alt** (novel, 2017), **Versenal** (poetry, 2016), **The Wordsmith** (short stories, 2016) and **Tandava** (poetry, 2018), co-authored with Mexican poet Silvia Siller.

Some of his poems have been included in several anthologies, such as **Voces del café** (Nueva York Poetry Press, 2018), **Intimate Portrait of Dominican Poets** (Taínos Editores, 2019), **New Century Poetic Voices**

(Kafla Intercontinental, India, 2016), **The Multilingual Anthology of The Americas Poetry Festival** (Artepoetica Press, 2015 and 2017), **Antología Poética (Vol. 1) Feria Internacional del Libro de la Ciudad de Nueva York** (Artepoetica Press, 2020), and **Narradores de Nueva York** (Artepoetica Press, 2022), among others.

Some of his short stories and poems have been selected for the following literary magazines: **Hybrido, Fuáquiti, Dualis Dualis, Nueva York Poetry Press Magazine, Azahar, The Latino Book Review Magazine, Trasdemar, Pleamar, Trazos,** and **The Official Lacuhe Gazette**.

He has translated works by Award-winning writers Elssie Cano (*Fiptisio '89*) and Kianny N. Antigua (*Children Literature*); and amazing works by the likes of Yorman Mejía, Belkis M. Marte, Loly Neira, Wanda Ferreiras and Carmen Romero, among many others.

In 2015, he founded **Books&Smith**, one of the fastest-growing Latino publishing houses in New York, with more than sixty titles up to date—among them, **Voces del vino** (Poetry, 2017), compiled by María Palitachi and winner of the *International Latino Book Awards* for Best Poetry Anthology and **Lo que el tiempo dejó** (novel, 2020) by renowned author Pedro Santana, winner of an Honorary Mention in the *International Latino Book Awards* for Best Romance Novel, 2021.

Smith has published books for some of the most important names in the Hispanic literary community, such as Poet Laureates César Sánchez Beras and Juan Matos, and Award-winning writers Kianny N. Antigua, Daniel Baruc Espinal, Jorge Paolantonio, Edwin Castillo, Elssie Cano, and María Palitachi, among many others.

He is also the creator of the renowned poetry event **Versos Estivales**, which takes place in New York City and focuses on cultural diversity and identity.

Index:

Other publications of Books&Smith:

My Childhood Memories

Belkis M. Marte

Aquí hubo una mujer

Kianny N. Antigua

Broken Crystals

Pedro Santana

La muerte y sus oficios

Daniel Baruc Espinal

El eterno día de Eufemio Obrero

Edwin Castillo

Fiptisio '89

Elssie Cano

www.booksandsmith.com

This work was completed in January 2022 under the supervision of Books&Smith Press. The e-book version of Through this strange window was self-published in March, 2021 via KDP.

booksandsmith@hotmail.com
www.booksandsmith.com
(917) 383-5195